The Boswell Kidnapping

Written by Keith Gray

Illustrated by Arianna Operamolla

Collins

Chapter 1

Half an hour ago, I'd been
eating breakfast and reading
a brilliant book about a robot
boy who had lasers in his
fingers and a nuclear bomb
instead of a heart. I'd decided it
was the best book I'd ever read.
I'd been thinking how great it would be to have
a nuclear bomb instead of a heart because no one
would dare mess with you in case you exploded.
But now I was chasing my dad up the wide stone steps
leading to Boswall & Son's department store. He was
rushing and panicking. And I reckoned he was
the person who looked most likely to explode.

"Come on, Alex," he shouted at me. "Hurry up,
lad. Move."

I'd been sitting at the kitchen table enjoying both my
book and my peanut butter on toast when Dad had
come downstairs.

"I hope you haven't eaten all the bread," was the first
thing he'd said. Then: "Who's the card for?"

"Mum," I'd told him. I'd propped the yellow envelope
up against the kettle, waiting for her to come home.
I knew the very first thing Mum did whenever she got in
from a night shift was make a pot of her favourite stinky,
weird herbal tea.

Dad had stood there in his old blue pyjamas
and groaned. He'd had a slice of bread in one hand
and was reaching out to plunk down the toaster button
with the other. But the bread never reached the toaster.
He'd charged back upstairs to pull some clothes over
his pyjamas and grab his car keys.

3

That's why we were racing up the steps of Boswall & Son's department store. It's the biggest shop in town and Dad reckoned it'd be impossible not to find Mum a present here.

"Let's just hope your mother appreciates all this fuss and bother we're having to go to, eh?" Dad growled. "I'm telling you, Alex, if there's ever a vote to have birthdays banned, I'll be first in the queue. I mean, *every* year? Who in their right mind enjoys celebrating getting older?"

"Yes, Dad," I said. "I don't know, Dad," I said.

"Getting another year older, what kind of an achievement is that meant to be? Everybody does it. It's not like you need qualifications, you don't have to have a certificate and it's not first prize in a competition. Why on earth do people want to keep celebrating all the time?"

"Yes, Dad," I said. "I don't know, Dad," I said.

To tell the truth, the only reason I'd remembered it was Mum's birthday was because she'd reminded me. The other day she'd said it was a pity Dad would be working on her birthday. She'd said she'd love to go to the cinema or to see a show or something. They'd both been working so hard recently they'd hardly seen each other, never mind had a night out together.

Mum's a nurse and Dad's a chef. It means they both work funny shifts and sometimes only keep in touch with each other through me. I'm son and messenger. I'm Alex, the answering machine.

When we got to Boswall's, Dad ran up the wide stone steps to the revolving door at the top. He was red-faced and panting. But when he looked at his watch, his face went even redder.

"Come on, Alex," he said, "I've got to be at the restaurant by eleven-thirty. We've got three new waiters starting today and I know for a fact that two of them are complete idiots. Hurry up, lad."

I hurried, really not wanting him exploding in public. That would be embarrassing.

7

Chapter 2

Boswall & Son's is not just the biggest shop in town,
it's the oldest too. It's a great grey grandad of a building.
Mum said she went here when she was little, and her
mum did too. It's as old and ancient as black and white TV.
But inside you can buy just about anything you can
think of. Like armchairs, basketballs and computers.
Or xylophones, yucca plants and zombie costumes.

   The first thing you notice after revolving through
the door is the smell. The make-up and perfume
department is on the ground floor. And it stinks.
There's so much thick perfume hanging in the air,
it coats the back of your throat like flowery paint.
I've also always been sure the scary, doll-faced saleswomen
who work here could give younger kids nightmares.

   What if it wasn't expensive perfume they were trying
to spray you with as you walked by, what if it was
a deadly virus? Just two fake-perfume squirts and you'd
be spreading the disease throughout the whole shop.
All of the other customers would catch it and die.
I'd read this brilliant book where stuff like that
really happened.

"Alex!"

I didn't realise Dad had been speaking to me.

"Stop daydreaming and help. What's your mother's favourite perfume?"

"You got her perfume for Christmas," I said.

He groaned. "Of course I did. You're right. And what did I get her for our anniversary? Was it a scarf?"

"Perfume," I said.

"Are you sure? The scarf was for Valentine's day, wasn't it?" He shook his head. "See what I mean, Alex? Birthdays, Valentine's, anniversaries, Christmases. How many celebrations do people want?"

I could see one of the saleswomen watching us from behind her counter. She was pretending to rearrange her glass bottles, displaying them as though they were as precious as Harry Potter's potions. I always got embarrassed when Dad ranted in public. There was also a security guard standing by the door, in his grey uniform that made him look like a foreign policeman.

"Your mother knows I love her," Dad went on, making me cringe even more. "It takes a lot more than buying expensive presents to prove you love someone. Of course your mother knows I love her."

I wondered if she'd still love him if she could see him waving his arms around Boswall's posh perfume department with his clothes pulled on over his pyjamas. I grabbed his sleeve to drag him through into the ground floor's main hall.

Underneath a high archway, the store opens out into a wide hall with escalators in the middle. All around are tall glass cabinets and long glass counters full of jewellery, watches, crystal ornaments – anything sparkly.

Dad walked beside the glass counters, leaning over and peering inside each of them as he went along. He grumbled and swore under his breath, tutting at the prices.

I lagged behind a little and pretended I wasn't with him. I had a glance around to make sure the other customers weren't looking at us, and I saw a boy of about my age on the escalator, heading up to the next floor. He had blond hair and was wearing sensible trousers, like school trousers, and a tee shirt that had come untucked. But the weird thing was, even though he had his back to me, I could tell he was crying. Maybe it was the way he was standing, all head-down and saggy shoulders.

None of the other customers seemed to notice him, or even care that he was crying.

I looked for Dad, but he'd wandered off towards a display of tinkly lampshades and wasn't paying any attention to me. So I followed the boy.

13

Chapter 3

I ran up the escalator's moving steps. It felt so important to me to find out what was wrong with this boy.

The first floor is the furniture department. There are lots of tables and beds and wardrobes. A few shoppers were testing out the sofas, but I couldn't see the boy anywhere. I made a guess, thinking he wouldn't want to hang around all this boring stuff and had probably gone through to look at the TVs and radios.
That's where I'd go.

But I spotted him walking in the opposite direction. He stopped and looked back over his shoulder. And the way he did it made me look back over my shoulder too.

Not that I could see anything special – just armchairs and stuff.

When I turned back, he'd gone again.

I had to run again. But he hadn't gone far. This department was all kitchen things like kettles and toasters and washing machines. Not what you'd call exciting. I didn't know why he'd want to be in here. But he seemed to be wandering around without looking at anything on the shelves. Half the time he looked at his feet.

I went up behind him and tapped him on the shoulder. He yelped and jumped about two metres in the air.

I laughed. I couldn't help it. "Sorry. I didn't mean – "

"What?" he said. "What?"

"I didn't mean, you know ...? To scare you."

He looked confused and embarrassed. Close up, I reckoned he was a year or two younger than me. He was a centimetre or two shorter than me, as well.

"Leave me alone."

"Honestly, I'm sorry," I said. "I just saw you, and saw you were crying."

He scowled at me. "So?" Then he stared at his feet again. "I'm allowed to cry, aren't I? And anyway, I'm not any more."

"Yes, you are."

He turned to hide his face, and I felt bad for embarrassing him so much.

"I'm sorry," I said again. "I just wondered why you were ... I thought I could help." I wasn't sure if that was true or not. But I couldn't help feeling curious about why he was crying.

"What do you care anyway?" he said.

I shrugged. "My name's Alex," I told him instead.

He pushed his floppy blond fringe out of his eyes and tried to wipe away some tears. "I'm Sam. And I don't care what you say, or if you think it's stupid to cry. I've lost my mum."

For a second I thought, "Is that all?" I didn't say it out loud, but he must have seen it on my face because he started sniffling again. And I felt mean. He was only young, seemed a bit wimpy too, and maybe he didn't know his way around Boswall's as well as I did.

"I'll help you find her," I said. "Come on, where did you last see her?"

He looked at me like I was mad.

"It's OK. I'm not going to kidnap you, am I?" I was smiling, trying to make a joke.

He gawped at me.

I tried to sound doubly friendly. The problem was, he had this look like he might start shouting, "Stranger danger!" at any second. A security guard in his grey uniform was hovering over by the display of microwaves and I got worried that Sam might try to get me arrested.

"What did she want to buy?" I asked.

He was staring at me like I was some kind of impossible chemistry test. He didn't know what to say. But he blinked, twice, and gave a big sniff.

"She ..." He scrubbed away the wetness from his cheeks. "Maybe she wanted clothes."

"That's upstairs, then," I said. "All the clothes are on the next floor." I beamed the biggest grin I had, feeling particularly pleased with myself for helping out.
"That's probably where she's going to be, isn't it? Do you want to go and look?"

He still seemed unsure. I beckoned for him to hurry up and at last he followed as I led the way.

Chapter 4

"What was your mum wearing?" I asked Sam when we
got to the second floor.

He looked worried, or maybe confused. "She's got
curly hair. It's really blonde and shiny."

I wondered if he was shy – or just not very clever.

"What colour coat did she have on?"

"Her favourite one is green. And it has a belt."

We walked up and down the aisles between the racks
of dresses looking for a blonde woman in a green coat.

"Maybe she's gone looking for you," I said to Sam.

He didn't answer. He wasn't saying much at all.
And he still seemed to spend more time looking at his
feet than for his mum.

I was starting to get worried about Dad, and knew
I should get back to him soon. He might even be able to
help – once he'd stopped shouting at me for running off.

Again, I noticed a security guard close by.
I reckoned he'd been following us around. It made
me angry. I wanted to go up to him and say, "I'm not
a shoplifter or a hoodie, OK? Just because I'm a kid it
doesn't mean I'm causing trouble." But then I thought
we could ask him if he'd seen a blonde lady in
a green coat.

Sam shook his head. "No. Don't ask him.
Please don't."

"Why not? I know he's only like a pretend policeman but – "

Sam just shook his head harder.

I sighed. He was being both weird and unhelpful now. It made me wonder if he wanted to find his mum. Or if she was even here at all.

"You sure you're not winding me up?" I asked. I used my extra couple of centimetres to tower over him. "Because if you're just having a laugh ..."

"No. Of course I'm not. Honest I'm not." He started crying again. "It's just ..."

Now I was feeling mean and embarrassed. I didn't want anybody thinking it was me making him cry. "Can't you stop crying?" I asked.

"I'm *not* crying," he lied.

"Look, we could easily find your mum if – "

"But she's not just lost, is she?" He wiped his wet face with his tee shirt.

I didn't understand what he was talking about.

"OK," he said. "I'll tell you."

"Tell me what?"

He looked over my shoulder, checking behind me – making me check over my shoulder too. But I didn't know what he was looking for.

"I can't tell you here." He pointed at the security guard. "We've got to get away from him."

I was about to ask why, but Sam ran off between the racks of clothes. I had to be quick not to lose him.

He ran up one aisle and down another. Then he turned on his heel and dashed towards the "Outdoors" department, full of rucksacks, hiking boots and tents. There were no other customers and no sales assistants either.

"Has he followed us?" Sam asked. "The grey policeman? Is he still there?"

"The security guard? He's over near the escalators," I said.

"We need somewhere he can't find us," Sam said.

A small tent had been set up on display in one corner. It looked like a big umbrella stuck to the floor. Sam went over and got down on his knees to poke his head inside. He checked to make sure I was coming, then scrambled in through the flap.

I crawled in after him. There was a funny, rubbery smell and Sam's face was tinted greenish because of the light coming through the tent's material. He wasn't crying any more, which I guessed was a good thing. But the way he was acting now was even weirder than weird.

"Tell me," I said. "What's going on?" I wondered if Sam was a shoplifter and needed someone to sneak his stolen goods out past the security guards. Or maybe he was on the run from a terrible prison where they tortured little kids; I'd read a book about that kind of prison once. Should I help him if he really had?

"You won't believe me," he said.

"Believe what?"

"But I'll tell you because you've already said it."

"Said what? What did I say?"

He leant forward and grabbed my arm. He gripped it hard enough to hurt. "My mum. She's not just lost. She's been kidnapped."

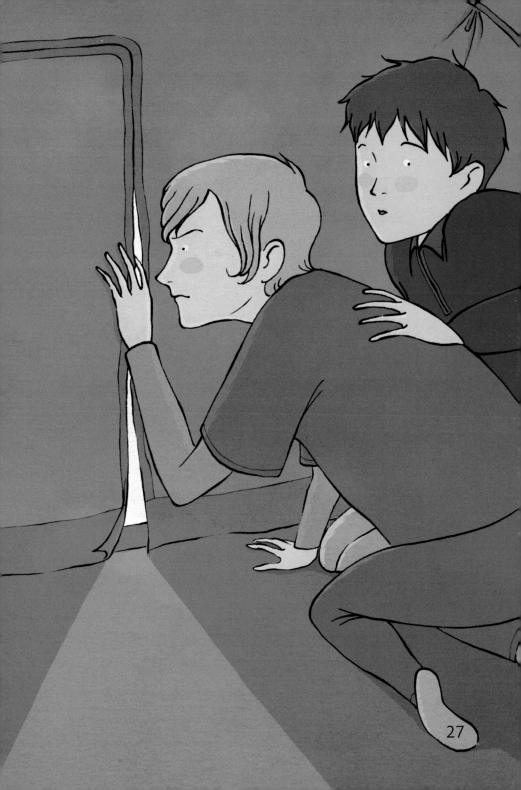

Chapter 5

"I knew you wouldn't believe me." Sam looked all tearful again.

"I never said I didn't." But then I didn't know what else to say. Was it true?

"They kidnapped my mum and now they want to kidnap me. That's why the grey policemen are following me."

"Do you mean the security guards?"

"They're only pretending to be security guards."

I was so confused. "But why – ?"

"Shhh!" Sam's eyes went wide and he waved at me to shut up.

There were footsteps close by. Heavy boots clomping on the tiled floor. We stayed silent, huddled in the little tent. The footsteps came closer. There was the thinnest gap in the flap of the tent where it wasn't zipped together. I could see shiny black boots and stiff trouser legs. It was a grey policeman. He was looking for us. He came so close that we could see his dark outline made fuzzy through the side of the tent.

He came so close that his dark outline loomed over us
on the curved roof. We both ducked down as if scared
of being touched by his shadow.

I was terrified of making a noise, even the tiniest little rustle.

I was scared to blink in case he could hear my eyelids clap.

I stayed totally, utterly, absolutely still. I didn't even breathe.

The sound of a walkie-talkie crackling almost made me leap out of my skin. Sam too, by the look of him.

The grey policeman said in a deep, rasping voice: "No, no kids here. Reckon he must have used the stairs. But there were two of them. It's only one we're after, right?"

Another voice came through the walkie-talkie but it crackled too much for me to be able to make out what it said.

"OK, I'll check," the grey policeman replied. He turned on the spot, having one last look around. Then he walked away, back under the arch.

Sam stared hard at me. "Now do you see?"

I nodded. My head was spinning. "Who are they? Who are the grey policemen?"

Sam lifted the tent's flap to look around, checking it was safe. "They're evil," he said.

"Are they spies?" I asked. "Are they chasing you because you're a spy too?"

He crawled out of the tent and I followed close behind. I had loads of questions but he put a finger to his lips to shush me. He crept past the display of rucksacks and hiking boots and pressed his back flat up against the wall by the side of the archway. He waved for me to keep out of sight. Then he leant around the archway, peeking over his shoulder and through into the main hall. He was acting like a spy now, that was for sure – all sneaky and stealthy.

"OK," he said. "It looks safe."

We sneaked back under the archway. It felt like
a hundred eyes were watching us. I was worried about
CCTV cameras, although when we scanned the ceiling
we couldn't spot any. Maybe we were lucky that
Boswall's was still so old-fashioned.

"Will you help me escape before the grey policemen find me?" Sam asked. "You heard that one say he was after me, didn't you?"

"But who are they? They look like foreign policemen to me. Or secret government agents."

"That's right," Sam said. "They're government agents. But it's a secret. So you've got to help me."

I nodded. My mind was in overdrive, trying to work out what to do. We needed a plan. "Maybe we can get you a disguise," I said. "There's fancy dress stuff in the toy department upstairs. We could get you a costume, or just change the way you look and – "

"Look out!" Sam shouted.

There was a grey policeman right behind me.

"Run!" Sam shouted.

I didn't need telling twice. I was hot on his heels as we charged headlong down the aisles between the racks of clothes.

35

Chapter 6

The grey policeman was right behind us. I could hear his heavy boots pounding on the floor, but nowhere near as loud as my heart was pounding in my chest.

Some customers yelped, some leapt out of our way, all were wide-eyed and stunned as we raced by. The shiny floor was slippery under my trainers. I skidded as I dodged around a tall rack of coats and almost fell. My feet skittered out from underneath me. But somehow I managed to stay upright and ran, ran, ran.

Sam was so quick for a little kid. He darted and ducked and weaved between customers and clothes racks. "This way!" he shouted.

We sprinted for the escalator. But there was another grey policeman trying to block us off. Sam went left. I went right. We dodged around him. He lurched towards me but I leapt out of his way. Again I nearly fell. Again I only just managed to stay on my feet. I ran, ran, ran.

I caught up with Sam. I was scared but he
looked terrified. I couldn't let the grey policemen
get him. Not like they'd got his mum. I saw a sign for
the stairs and the fire exit.

"This way," I shouted, gasping for breath.
"Sam! This way."

We banged through the double doors, slamming them back on their hinges. We ran down, watching our feet, one hand against the wall so we didn't fall, leaping three and four steps at a time. There was a short landing where the stairs turned a corner and there was a red door with "Staff Only" written on it. We could hear the grey policemen following us down, their boots so loud above us in the echoing stairwell. I grabbed Sam and pulled him through the red door.

It was a narrow cupboard with shelves on either side. I could smell bleach. There was a mop and bucket and a large yellow sign leaning against the wall that said "Cleaning in progress". Under the shelves at the back was a space just about big enough for the two of us to squeeze into. We crammed ourselves in tight and pulled the cleaning sign in front of us.

Then we held our breath.

But the boot-steps of the grey policemen didn't even stop. They ran straight down the stairs, thudding all the way.

Even so, we didn't move. We didn't dare. We stayed there until our hearts had stopped thumping. And it may have only been five minutes, but it felt like five hours.

Chapter 7

We sat on the floor of the cleaning cupboard and talked in whispers. We had to come up with a plan.

"They'll be guarding all the doors," I said. "And the fire exits. You definitely need a disguise."

Sam didn't look keen.

"They're looking for a small kid with blond hair and school trousers, right?" I said. "So we just have to make you look different. I read this book where this man was a master of disguise. He could rob banks, assassinate people, sneak into top-secret buildings – anything. It was brilliant."

"A master of disguise?" Sam asked.

"Well, he wasn't actually a *man* man," I admitted. "He was this alien – a shape-shifter from a weird planet. But he was very cool. He could disguise himself to look like anything that was alive. So even animals, but not cars or guns."

Sam just shrugged. "I wish I could shape-shift."

I cracked open the cleaning cupboard door and put my eye to the gap. "All clear."

We crept out on to the stairs, listening hard, ready to run at the slightest sound of grey policemen.

I pointed up the stairs, Sam nodded, and we made our way to the top floor on tiptoes.

When we got to the toy department I went first. There were loads of people hanging around the computer games, and some others over by the remote-controlled cars. There was a granny and grandad looking at board games, but no one at the shelves with all the party decorations and fancy dress stuff. And no grey policemen.

"It's safe," I told Sam and beckoned for him to follow.

It was only when we looked at the fancy dress costumes that I began to think my plan might not work.

"It might be hard to sneak out looking like Batman or Scooby Doo," Sam said.

"We just need to make you look different somehow."

There was a shelf of wigs and fake beards. I reached down a curly black wig and held it out to him. "Just try it," I said. "We'll sneak you out and then get my dad to take you somewhere safe."

He took the wig but didn't put it on. "Will you be in a lot of trouble with your dad?"

I shrugged. Then nodded. "He'll probably want to know what's going on. He'll want to know who the grey policemen are and why they've kidnapped your mum."

Sam was quiet.

"Why won't you even tell me?" I asked.

He plucked at the plastic hairs on the cheap wig.

"Because I'm scared you won't believe me."

I couldn't help feeling angry. "What do you mean, won't believe you? I'm helping you, aren't I? I've been chased by grey policemen too, haven't I?"

I'd frightened him by shouting. His eyes darted here, there and everywhere.

I lowered my voice to a whisper. "You've got to tell me. Is your mum a spy?" This was my best guess. "Is she spying for another country?"

He shook his head. Then nodded. Then shook his head again.

I was mystified. "What?"

Sam was flustered. He started to get all tearful again. "The grey policemen are government agents, just like you say. But my mum's not a spy."

"What is she then?"

Sam whispered even quieter than me.

"What?" I asked. "She's ...?"

"An alien," he repeated.

I stared at him, my mouth hanging open.

"It's true, it's true," he said. "She's from another planet, and the grey policemen found out. That's why they've kidnapped her."

I didn't know what to say. "But ..." I didn't know what to think.

"She was different from everyone else. Really special and different. And that's why she's been taken away."

This was crazy. Wasn't it? "If your mum ...? Are you also ...?"

He shook his head. "No, no. My dad's human."

"But you're still half alien?"

"I'm half boy," he said. "I'm half my dad, but half my mum too."

Wow! Aliens! My head was spinning. My thoughts were crashing. Was it true?

"Yes, you see?" Sam grabbed at my arm. "That's what's wrong. That's why I want my mum back. I'm only half a boy without her, aren't I?" He clutched at me and tugged on my arm, desperate for me to understand. "Don't you see?"

I still didn't know what to say. But there was something in his eyes, some look that made me believe he believed. No matter how crazy it all sounded, Sam believed it.

But then a voice thundered behind me: "Alex! Where on earth have you been? I've been searching all over for you." I turned to see Dad storming towards me across the toy department.

I also saw he wasn't alone. He had two grey policemen with him.

I didn't stop to wonder what my dad was doing with grey policemen. All I could think about was Sam not getting caught. "Run!" I shouted. "Run!"

But there was another man behind Sam. A tall man with floppy blond hair.

"Whoa, there," he said as he gathered Sam up in his arms. "Whoa, Sam."

Chapter 8

There was a lot of shouting in the fancy dress section of the toy department at Boswall & Son's. Dad did most of it.

"But – " I said for about the hundredth time. "But – "

Dad was bellowing all these questions at me and then not giving me time to answer. Where had I been? What on earth was this he'd been told about me chasing around the women's clothing department like a hooligan? Didn't I know he'd had the security guards searching the whole shop for me?

If he'd paused for breath for even a second, I'd have answered as honestly as I could. Even the two security guards looked shocked and awkward. He was drawing quite a crowd.

The tall, blond man who was still hugging Sam stepped forward. "Hello there," he said. He held out his hand for Dad to shake. "I'm Robert Gibson, Sam's father." He smiled, which only seemed to bewilder Dad.

I tried to catch Sam's eye but he was staring at his feet.

"I think it's my son who owes you and Alex an apology," Robert Gibson said. "Sam's been having a bit of trouble lately. His mother, my wife, she died just last week." He took a breath. "And, well, I'm afraid we're both having difficulty coming to terms with it." He held Sam tightly.

I'd added it up in my head now. Sam had said he'd "lost" his mum. He'd only talked about kidnap, or acted like a spy, or even mentioned aliens, after I'd said something first. I'd been letting him lead me along without even realising it. And the security guards had been looking for me, not him.

Dad had been cut short. He was struggling for words. "His mother? Your wife? Oh, I'm ... No, no, I'm sure it's us who should ..." He was carrying a Boswall's bag and I guessed my mum's birthday present was inside. He gripped the handles so tightly his knuckles went white.

Robert Gibson asked the security guards, "There's no real harm done, is there? No actual damage?" They shook their heads. "Can you apologise, Sam?"

Sam looked up at them from beneath his blond fringe. "I'm very sorry for the trouble I've caused in your shop."

They didn't look happy, but they nodded and walked away, waving the onlookers back as they went.

"And to Alex and his father?" Robert Gibson asked.

Sam looked at Dad. "I hope I haven't got Alex into trouble. He was really nice to me."

Dad mumbled something like, "He's not in trouble." And I hoped he meant it.

Sam's eyes were heavy and wet but he held the tears back. "Sorry, Alex. Thank you for being nice to me."

"I'm sorry I didn't understand," I said. "I hope you'll be OK."

Sam tried to smile. Then he lost the fight with his tears and his father had to gather him up as he wept.

We said goodbye. Dad put a hand on my shoulder and steered me away. We headed downstairs. I tried to explain everything as well as I could. What Sam had said at the end was playing on my mind.

"Sam said he was only half a boy without his mum," I told Dad. "Do you think that's true?"

We revolved through the main door and back outside to the top of the stone steps.

"I think you're always going to be made up of both your mum and dad, no matter where they are, don't you?" he said.

I nodded. I guessed he was right.

I asked him what he'd bought Mum for her birthday. He looked at the bag in his hand as if he'd forgotten about it. With a sigh he dumped it in the nearest litter bin.

He said, "As punishment for this little escapade, I think you can buy her a present. You're paying for a baby-sitter, agreed?"

I didn't understand.

"While I'm going to let the restaurant know that I'm not coming in to work today. It's my wife's birthday. And I really think that's cause for celebration, don't you?"

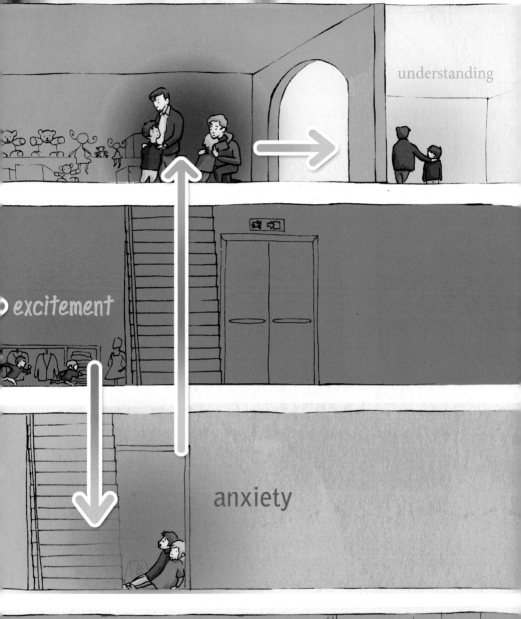

understanding

excitement

anxiety

55

Ideas for guided reading

Learning objectives: understand underlying themes, causes and points of view; use oral techniques to present engaging narratives; improvise using a range of drama strategies to explore themes such as fears

Curriculum links: Citizenship: Moving on

Interest words: kidnapping, queue, security guard, escalators, aisles, walkie-talkie, CCTV, agents

Resources: whiteboard, ICT

Getting started

This book can be read over two or more guided reading sessions.

- Read the blurb and look at the cover together. Suggest questions these create for the reader, e.g. *I wonder who is trying to kidnap them ...*

- Ask children to predict answers to these questions, and explain their reasons for these. Write their ideas on the whiteboard for later.

- Ask children if they have been in a department store and discuss any experiences they have had there. What did they think of it? Did anything strange ever happen while they were there?

Reading and responding

- Read the first chapter together as a group and discuss the relationship between Alex and his dad. Do they have a similar relationship with a parent or guardian?

- Ask children to read quietly until the end of the book, making notes of questions they have at each chapter and any answers they have for these by the end.

- Return to the predictions on the whiteboard and see if any of them were correct or similar to the events in the book and why.

Returning to the book

- Turn to pp16-17 and consider how each character is feeling at this point. Discuss points in the story where they are both feeling the same emotion, and points where their emotions are different, and why this could be.